I Have the Heart of a
WARRIOR
Affirmations to Empower Kids

Written by
Leslie Lew

Illustrated by
Seyma Arslan

Dedication

For Phoenix and Amaya,

You are my greatest teachers and fiercest loves, living proof that courage runs in our blood. This book is my heart poured onto these pages—a legacy of strength, love, and the warrior spirit within you. May you always know your power, carry these words forward, and inspire the warriors who come after you.

Copyright © Leslie Lew, 2025
Edited by: Jveria Gauhar
Illustrated by: Şeyma Arslan
Published by: Global Bookshelves International, LLC
ISBN: 978-1-957242-24-8 (paperback)
LCCN: 2024923787

Printed in the United States of America.

To comment on this book, send an email to the author at leslie@reclaimingyourcourage.com.

All rights reserved. No part of this publication may be reproduced, stored in a retrieval system, or transmitted in any form or by any means, electronic, mechanical, photocopying, recording, or otherwise, without prior written permission of the publisher.

Foreword

Dear parent/caregiver,

As you hold this book in your hands, I invite you to embark on a journey of empowerment and connection with your child. Your role as a parent or caregiver is crucial in shaping their beliefs, building their confidence, and igniting their inner strength. Your words are powerful tools that can guide them towards a positive self-belief.

As you turn the pages, may the affirmations on each page serve as the words you needed to hear as a child growing up. As you read, please encourage your child to repeat the affirmations after you, turning it into a joyful and interactive experience. For example, when your child feels scared, you can say, "You are a warrior; you can face this fear with courage."

Let us raise a generation of brave warriors who shine bright and soar high, knowing they are loved, valued, and not alone. Remember, these affirmations are not just words; they are seeds of confidence and self-belief that you are planting in your child's heart.

—Leslie Lew

I have the heart of a warrior.
But what is a warrior?

A warrior is a very brave friend.
They don´t need special clothes or masks to be strong.
They are like superheroes but face their fears with a big heart, just like yours.

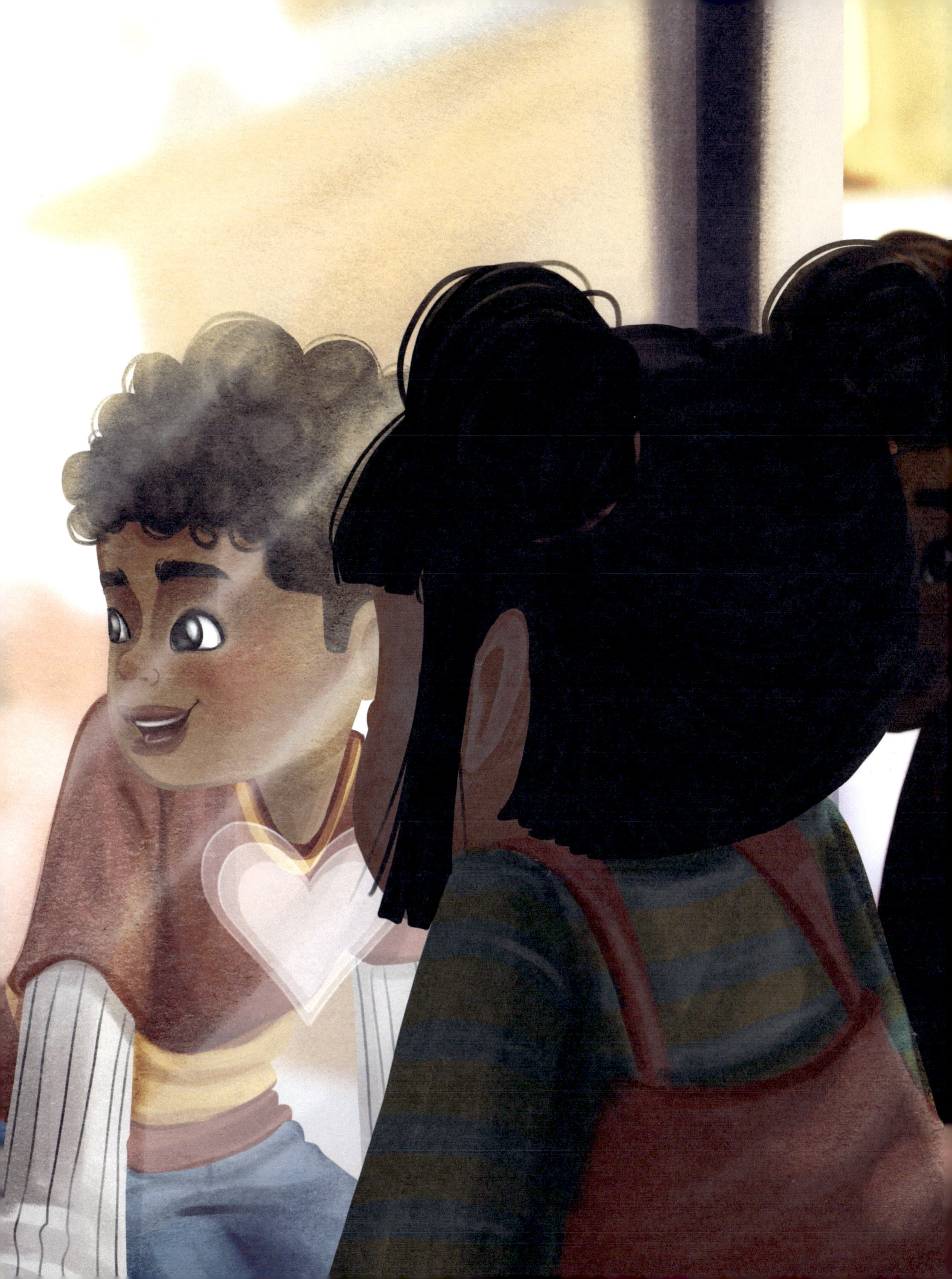

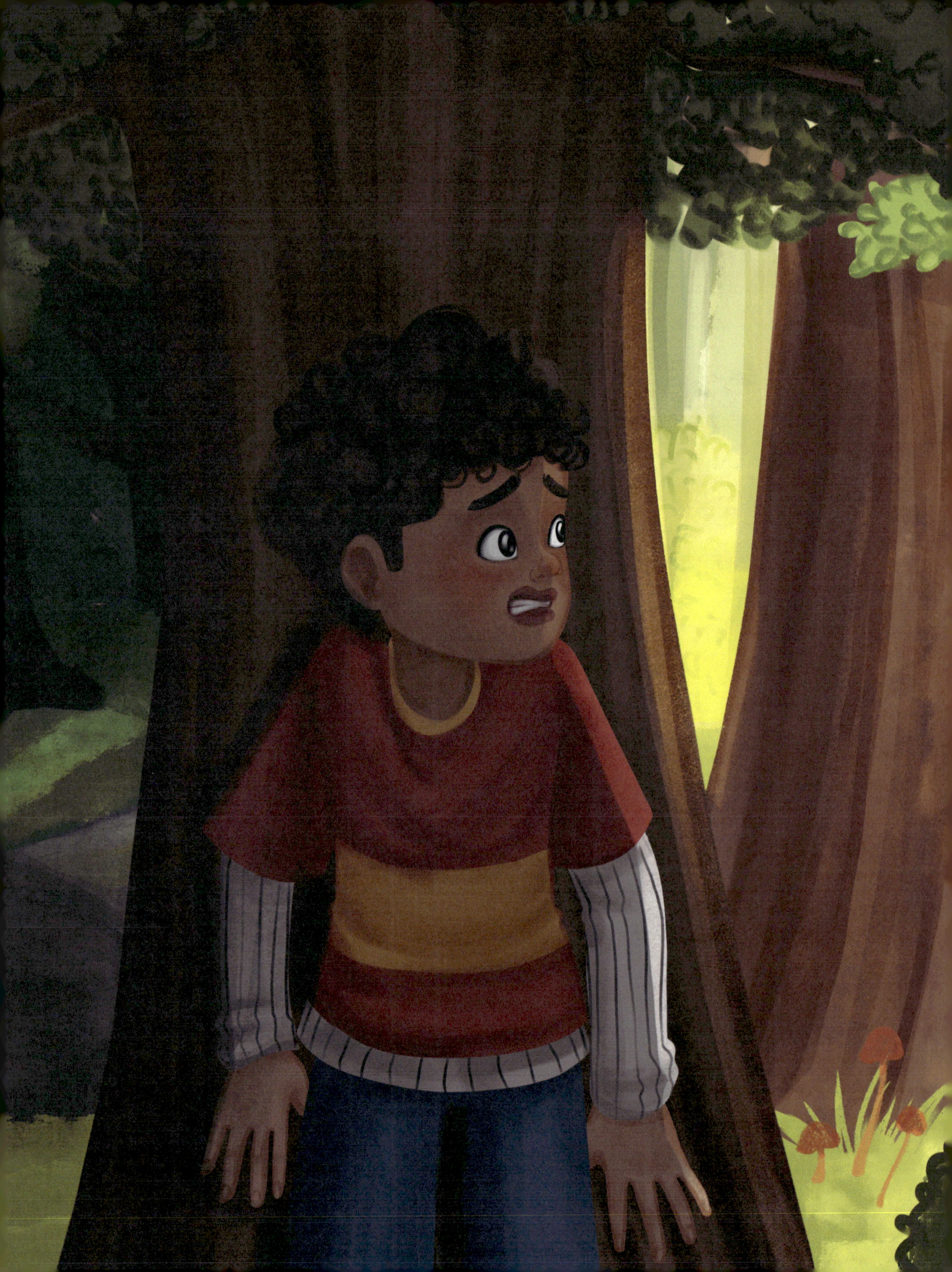

A warrior doesn't get scared easily because they have something special. They have courage.

This makes them strong and brave, just like you.

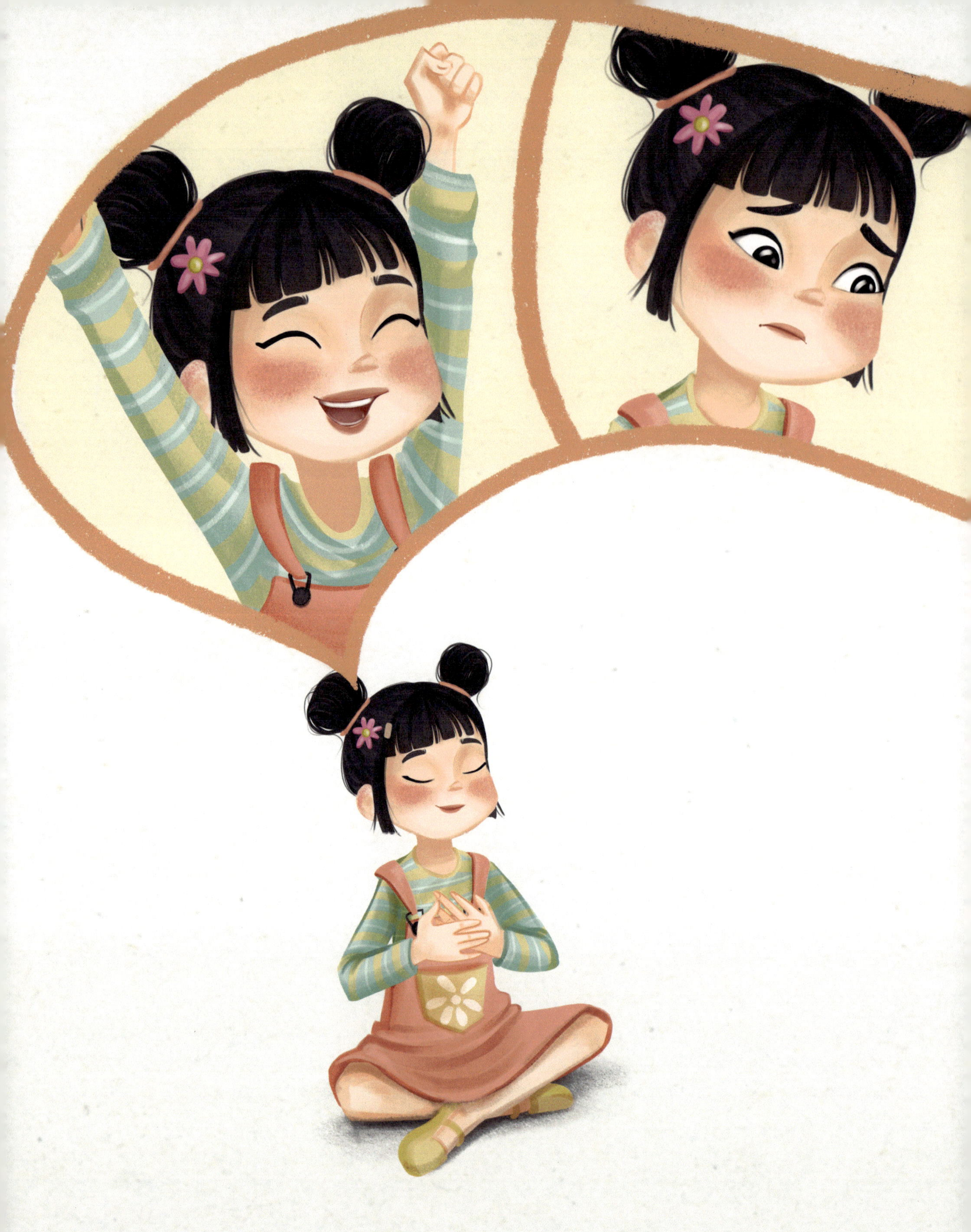

A warrior feels all sorts of feelings—
happy, sad, excited, or even scared.

Feeling these things makes them stronger.

A warrior believes in themselves.

They keep trying and never give up,
even when things are tough.

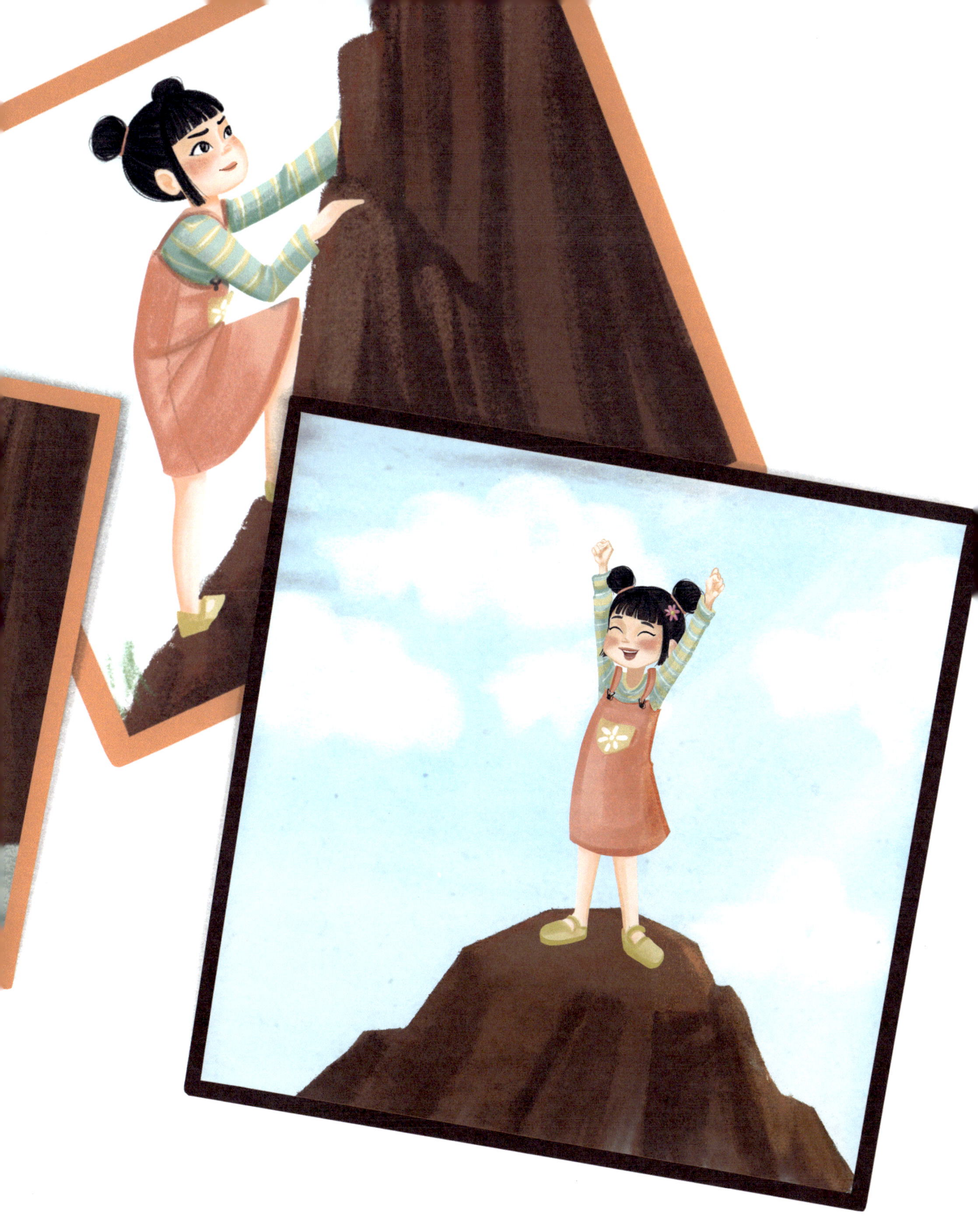

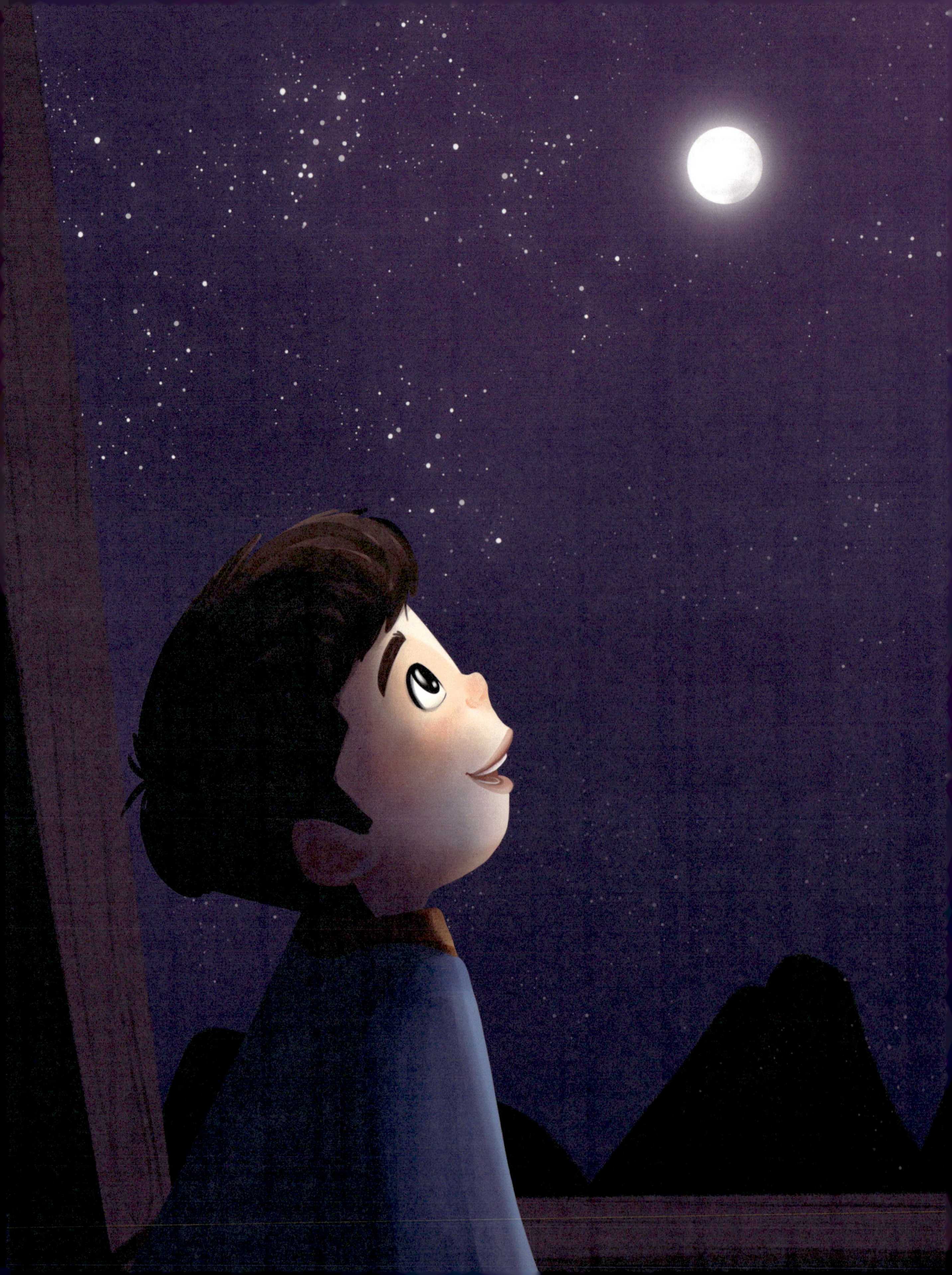

Within every warrior, there's a tiny spark that makes them shine like a star.

When you feel these powerful feelings, it's time to light that spark by saying the affirmations in **bold.**

Ready? Let's turn the page.

When I feel alone, and
no one seems to understand,
I remember I am a warrior.

I stay true to myself.

Being different is okay, and I can
face anything with courage.

**I can find good company
within myself.**

I am never truly alone.

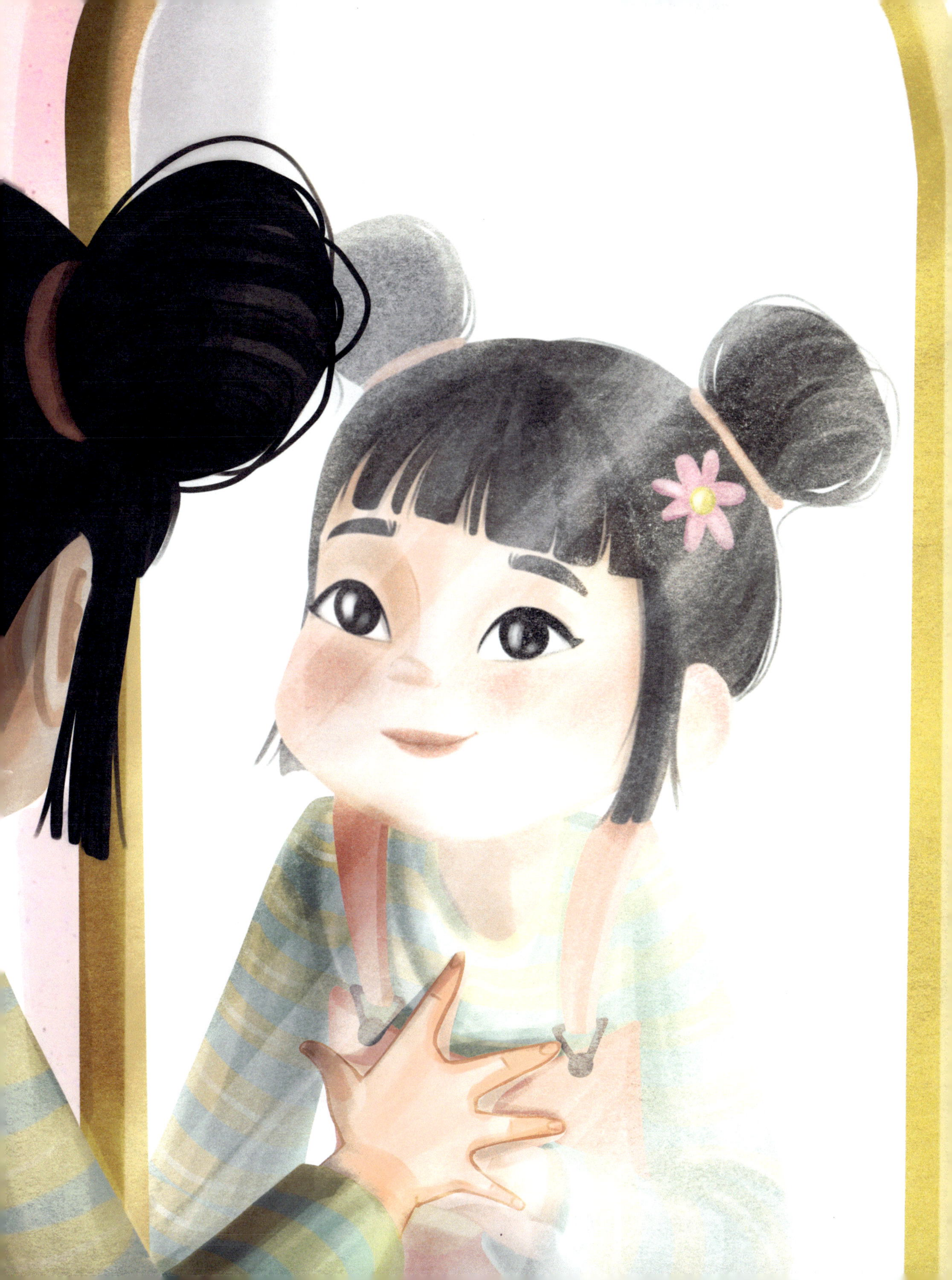

When I feel like I don't get the math problem, I remind myself that everyone learns at their own pace. I am a warrior. I try. I learn. I strive. I don't give up. I am a warrior. I will grow (when I allow myself grace). **I say, 'I am a warrior. I can figure this out. I can achieve anything.'**

When I feel different, I remember that beauty shines from my heart. I am a warrior; I love what makes me different from everyone else. Warriors must have thick skin.

I tell myself, `I am strong. I am confident.´

When I feel weak, I remind myself that I must grow.
**I rise when I fall. I rest when I break. I try when I fail.
And I must grow stronger every day.** Warriors come in different forms, shapes, and sizes. I believe in myself.

When I feel alone and unloved, I remind myself that love is always around me. **I am a warrior, and I hold onto the love within me. I am worthy of love, and I choose caring friends to surround me**—friends just like you.

When I see someone struggling, I help because warriors face every challenge, even if it means drying someone's tears. If they feel alone, I remind them they're strong. If they feel different, I remind them of their beauty. If they feel weak, I remind them not to give up. If they feel unloved, I remind them of the love around them.

I am a warrior. I help others in need. Together, we can overcome anything and find comfort knowing we're never truly alone.

Daily Affirmations that I can say every day:

I am a warrior; I stay true to myself.
I am a warrior; I have good company within myself.
I am a warrior; **I keep trying and learning.**

I can figure this out. **I can achieve anything.**

I am a warrior; **I believe in myself.**
I am a warrior; I must grow stronger every day.
I am a warrior; I hold onto the love within myself.

I am worthy of love.

I am a warrior; I help others in need.
I am a warrior; **I am ready.**

Leslie Lew, widely known as the "Warrior," stands as a global speaker, humanitarian, and women's self-defense coach. Her dynamic career is marked by significant accolades, including recognition from the Washington DC Chronicle News as one of the "Global Women to Watch in 2024" and receiving the prestigious 2022 Asian Woman Trailblazer award.

Leslie, the visionary founder of Reclaiming Your Courage and co-founder of the global women's movement Warrior Queens Rise, is not just a champion for women's rights, but a woman deeply rooted in the values of love, courage, and community. Her personal mission is to empower women, equipping them with the tools and confidence to stand against gender-based violence.

A devoted mother and wife, Leslie seamlessly balances her personal and professional life. Her expertise in martial arts, evidenced by her status as a two-time black belt, underscores her commitment to self-defense and empowerment.

Stay connected to Leslie's work: www.reclaimingyourcourage.com.

Şeyma Arslan was born in Turkiye in 1997. Since childhood, she has had a passion for drawing. She developed this talent by attending various courses and graduated with honors from the Faculty of Fine Arts, Department of Graphic Design. She has illustrated many stories for various publications and had the opportunity to work on storyboards for several animated shows in Turkiye. While actively working in the graphic design sector, she continues to engage in various activities within the field of illustration.

In her free time, she enjoys exploring new flavors and places, and she also works on Islamic calligraphy to both relax and develop her artistic skills.

She strives to ensure that her drawings are meaningful and serve a purpose. For this reason, she greatly enjoys illustrating children's books and aims to create joyful memories for many children through her work.

For additional resources, visit http://globalbookshelves.com/warrior.

Made in the USA
Columbia, SC
10 May 2025